The Legend of the Dog Warrior

战犬传奇

By David Saechao

Illustrated by Calvin Saephanh

ISBN-13: 978-1541201460

ISBN-10: 1541201469

For Justin, Shanty, and Nathan

Special thanks to Kenny Chao, Maggie Zhai, and our families and friends for their support.

Long ago, in a tiny village, a puppy fell from the sky.

The villagers were curious and wondered why the heavens had sent down a cuddly looking pup. They gathered around it to get a peek at the mysterious little creature.

Master Yang, the village leader, was among the crowd. He picked up the pup and cradled it in his hand. Hmm, what to do with a dog that has fallen from the sky, he thought to himself, as he stared into the pup's gleaming eyes.

His wife, Mrs. Yang, knew exactly what they needed to do. "We must raise it as our own," she suggested. "We may never know why it was sent here, but it is our responsibility now."

"But my dear wife…," cried Master Yang.

"But yes!" she quickly interrupted him.

"Very well," replied Master Yang. "I hereby name you Pan Hu. I will teach you how to speak, read, and write. How to be kind. How to be a great warrior. People all across China will soon know your name."

Siec

Two years went by, and Pan Hu had grown up fast.

He had learned the highest levels of kung fu, mastering secret techniques that had been passed down for generations.

Hietc

All of the children loved Pan Hu and had fun watching him leap great heights, kicking and punching. They even gave him a nickname. He came to be known as Pan Hu, the Dog Warrior.

The adults loved Pan Hu too. They enjoyed having intelligent conversations with him and were fascinated by how smart he had become.

Nduoh

It was not long before everyone in the kingdom heard about Pan Hu. When word reached the capital city, King Gao was astonished and ordered Pan Hu to be a guest at the palace. "Bring me the talking dog!"

Master Yang and his wife were sad that the King had ordered Pan Hu to live at the palace. They had come to love Pan Hu as a son and did not know when their little dog warrior would return. The loving couple hugged Pan Hu and said a tearful goodbye.

"Pan Hu, do you know why you are here?" asked the King.

"Yes, King Gao," Pan Hu puffed proudly. "I am here to be your greatest warrior."

The King broke out in hysterical laughter and almost fell over his throne. "You will not be my greatest warrior. You will be my pet dog!"

The palace erupted in laughter. Pan Hu bowed his head n embarrassment. He spotted a dark corner and hobbled his way there to find comfort.

As the laughter faded, he was escorted to his bedroom.

That night, Pan Hu cried himself to sleep.

The next morning Pan Hu was summoned to the palace. He was met by a jubilant gathering of the King's family. In attendance was the King's only daughter, the beautiful Princess Bingbing.

"Pan Hu, tell us a joke or do something funny. I want to be entertained," demanded the King.

Pan Hu was not sure what to do. "But King Gao, I don't know any jokes. I only know kung fu."

"Did your master not teach you any?"

Ziepc Hmz

As King Gao was about to speak, the palace doors suddenly swung open. A soldier hurried into the palace, carrying a scroll. He kneeled down beside Pan Hu and unrolled the scroll to reveal an urgent message from General Sun.

My lord King Gao, I am sorry to inform you that the kingdom is under attack. The evil General Wu's barbarian armies of the West have taken over three of our cities and are headed toward the palace. Please send help. And hurry!

The King began to feel the stirrings of panic. He stood up from his throne and paced around, wondering what he should do.

"Call my greatest warriors to the palace!" he ordered.

Shortly, five of the King's best warriors trickled into the palace. "I need one of you to lead our army and defeat General Wu."

The warriors stood in silence. They were afraid of General Wu, for every living soul in China knew the power of the Western barbarians. The evil general was known for destroying entire cities and villages.

The King, desperate, asked his warriors once again. "Who will lead our army and defeat General Wu and bring me his sword?" There was still no sound. The King sat down on his throne and sunk into disappointment.

Princess Bingbing, disappointed in the warriors as well, could bear the silence no longer. "Okay, I promise that if one of you defeats General Wu, you can marry me."

Princess Bingbing was the most beautiful woman in the ingdom, and the King knew that many warriors would love to narry her.

"Oh great king, let me lead your army."

"Who is it that speaks?" asked the King, as he looked round the palace.

"Why it's me, Pan Hu, the Dog Warrior."

The King was not happy about Pan Hu leading the army, ut he had no other choice. He nodded approvingly.

Suddenly, Princess Bingbing had second thoughts about the promise she made. "Dad, even if Pan Hu defeats General Wu, I am not going to marry a dog."

"My dear princess. We are under attack. You must honor your promise."

The Princess glanced at Pan Hu and abruptly left the palace in protest.

Pan Hu met his soldiers outside the palace gates. The small army was made up of only a few thousand soldiers. He could not help but notice the fear in their eyes.

"Fight with me!" he roared. "Don't be scared of General Wu. He will regret ever meeting us." The soldiers cheered and raised their swords, as they prepared to march west.

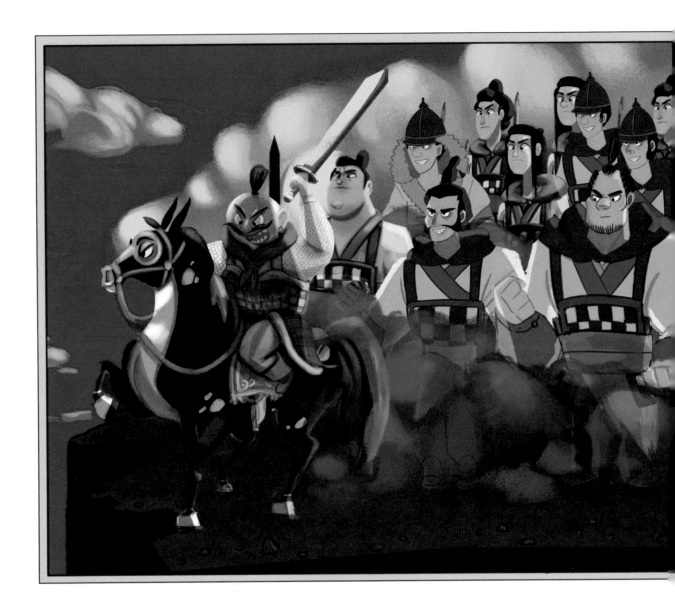

General Wu led a massive army of soldiers. Their footsteps created a thunderous tremble that brought fear to many.

Pan Hu could wait no longer. The Dog Warrior dashed forth and inspired his soldiers to follow him into battle.

The two armies clashed, and it was not long before Pan Hu met General Wu on the battlefield. It was a duel to be remembered for ten thousand years.

General Wu was the bigger, stronger warrior, and his strength forced Pan Hu to the ground. "You have lost Pan Hu," snarled the General. "Give up. You are just a dog, not a warrior."

"Not if I have anything to say about it." Pan Hu got up quickly and subdued General Wu. "Yes, I have your sword now!"

General Wu's soldiers noticed that their leader had fallen. "Retreat! Retreat!" yelled one of the soldiers.

Pan Hu's army was victorious. All of his soldiers rejoiced as they watched their enemy flee.

Pan Hu and his army marched back to the palace and was welcomed by a grand celebration. Thousands of people chanted, "Pan Hu! Pan Hu! Pan Hu!"

Approaching the palace steps, Pan Hu walked up to meet Princess Bingbing. He looked at his soon-to-be bride. "My lady, please don't worry about my appearance. I am blessed by the gods."

"But Pan Hu, you're a dog. Do you expect a princess to marry a dog?"

"Yes, princess," Pan Hu replied. He stretched out his arms and looked toward the sky. A beam of light from the heavens connected with Pan Hu and knocked him to the ground.

The Princess, fearing that Pan Hu might have been killed, burst into tears. Much to her surprise, Pan Hu's face no longer resembled a dog. He had been transformed into a handsome young man.

The next day Pan Hu and Princess Bingbing were married and ready to start a new life together. The King had given them land to the south and offered Pan Hu a new title. The Dog Warrior, for his courageous efforts, had become King Pan.

Many years later, Princess Bingbing would give birth to twelve beautiful children, six boys and six girls.

King Pan was a proud husband and father.

A new kingdom was born.

Made in the USA
Middletown, DE
06 November 2020